SALAMANDERS

written by
EMERY BERNHARD

pictures by
DURGA BERNHARD

HOLIDAY HOUSE • NEW YORK

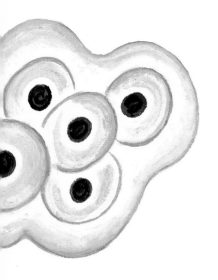

Jacket and book design by Durga Bernhard

Library of Congress Cataloging-in-Publication Data
Bernhard, Emery.
Salamanders / written by Emery Bernhard ; illustrated by Durga
Bernhard. — 1st. ed.
p.   cm.
ISBN 0-8234-1148-6
1. Salamanders—Juvenile literature.   [1. Salamanders.]
I. Bernhard, Durga, ill.   II. Title.
QL668.C2B38   1995   94-15306   CIP   AC
597.6'5—dc20

Key to Front & Back Covers
1. **Fire Salamander**
2. **Blue-Spotted Salamander**
3. **Valdina Farms Salamander**
4. **Orange-Striped Crocodile Newt**
5. **Tiger Salamander**
6. **Marbled Newt**
7. **Northern Red Salamander**
8. **Silvery Salamander**
9. **Flatwoods Salamander**

Title page: Marbled Newt

For Jim Gardner,
who helped make
this book possible,
and who loves salamanders.

CRESTED
NEWT

Special thanks to herpetologist and science educator Joe Martinez, M.A.,
Ph.D. candidate at Boston University,
for his comments on the text and artwork.

TWO-LINED
SALAMANDER

It is a foggy, rainy night in late March. The snow has melted, and the ground is soft and soggy. There is just enough moonlight to see the green tips of new skunk-cabbage leaves poking through the wet earth.

BROKEN-STRIPED NEWT

MABEE'S SALAMANDER

Hundreds of slippery creatures are moving about the woods.
They crawl through leaves and climb over rocks and wiggle
under logs. They are salamanders, making their way toward the
pools and ponds where they will mate and lay eggs.

SALAMANDER FOOT   LIZARD CLAW

Salamanders are often mistaken for lizards, but they do not have the lizard's claws and scaly skin.

Salamanders are amphibious. They spend part of their lives in water and part on land.

Like all amphibians, salamanders are cold-blooded. Their bodies are the same temperature as their surroundings.

The Tiger Salamander is sometimes seen at night after a heavy rain. Up to 15 inches in length, it is the largest of all the salamanders that dwell on land.

Salamanders breathe and drink through their tender, moist skin. They must keep their skin moist at all times. They cannot survive if they remain for too long in the hot, drying sun or in the freezing cold.

Most salamanders live in cool, damp places. They hide during the day under leaves, rocks, logs, mud, or in other animals' abandoned burrows—and come out at night or on rainy days.

Many salamanders return to the same pool every year to breed. During mating season, male salamanders deposit packets of sperm in or near the water. Each type of male salamander has a courtship dance for attracting mates. Some coil around the female, others shove or nuzzle her. Males also give off a special smell that guides females to their sperm. The female then takes the sperm into her body.

After mating, female salamanders lay their fertilized eggs in ponds, pools, or in other wet and sheltered places. They lay them one at a time or in clusters or strings of up to 150. Salamander eggs are covered with a clear, sticky jelly that swells after the eggs are laid. The jelly holds the eggs in place, often sticking to underwater twigs and stems or to the underside of damp rocks and rotting logs.

GROWING SALAMANDER LARVAE
VISIBLE INSIDE EGGS

If the egg clusters are laid under the water, they may turn green from a plant-like growth called algae. The waste products from the tiny salamanders growing in the eggs help feed the algae, and the algae in turn produce some of the oxygen that the growing salamanders need to breathe.

Many salamander eggs are eaten by birds, snakes, fish, and raccoons.

SPOTTED
SALAMANDER LARVA

Salamanders hatch after a few weeks. A baby salamander, called a larva, has a flat tail used for swimming and feathery gills for taking oxygen from the water. It stalks tiny worms and water insects, snatching them with its wide mouth.

Not all salamanders are born in the water. Salamanders that hatch on land are born with legs and without gills. They breathe through their skin, although some have lungs for breathing as well.

The Spotted Salamander has no spots when it first crawls up on land. Its yellow spots will appear after several weeks.

Most salamanders that begin their lives in the water will lose their gills, develop lungs for breathing, and grow legs before moving onto the land. Unlike frogs and toads, salamanders do not lose their tails as they grow and change. These tailed amphibians develop from a larva into an adult over a period of several months. This is called metamorphosis.

When they have become adults, salamanders leave the water and begin their life on land.

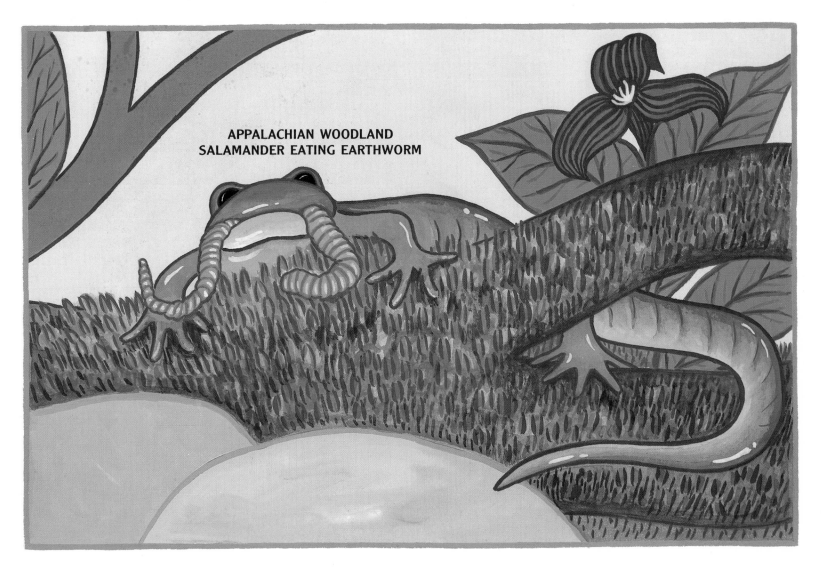

APPALACHIAN WOODLAND
SALAMANDER EATING EARTHWORM

Salamanders hunt for earthworms, slugs, spiders, and insects.
When a salamander sees or smells food, it stalks carefully, moving slowly toward its prey. As soon as the salamander is close
enough, it makes a quick grab, snatching its victim with its
jaws.

The diet of large salamanders may include small snakes, baby
mice, and tiny frogs.

MOUNTAIN DUSKY
SALAMANDER

Adult salamanders are hunted by larger predators, such as raccoons and opossums. Some salamanders are poisonous to eat, and have brightly colored skin that warns predators to keep away. Others hide from enemies by using their skin colors and markings to blend in with their surroundings. This is called camouflage.

The tiny Pygmy Salamander can measure as little as 1½ inches from head to tail.

Salamanders rest quietly in very cold or dry weather, finding shelter until spring or until the return of the rainy season. The Northern Red Salamander often spends the winter sheltered under layers of dead leaves.

Salamanders range in length from 1 inch to 5 feet. They vary in color and markings. Salamanders can live up to thirty years in the wild, and have been known to survive for fifty-five years in zoos or as pets.

There are salamanders that climb trees, others that burrow in mud, and some that never leave water. Of about 360 kinds of salamanders in the world, over 100 types live in North America.

SPOTTED
SALAMANDER

North American salamanders can be divided into seven main groups: <u>Mole Salamanders</u>, <u>Newts</u>, <u>Giant Salamanders</u>, <u>Amphiumas</u>, <u>Sirens</u>, <u>Mudpuppies</u> and <u>Waterdogs</u>, and <u>Lungless Salamanders</u>.

MARBLED
SALAMANDER

Mole Salamanders are born in the water and live on land as adults. Like moles, they are often busy tunneling their underground homes.

The Spotted Salamander and the Marbled Salamander are two common Mole Salamanders found east of the Rockies. Spotted Salamanders can grow to almost 10 inches in length, while Marbled Salamanders are 3½ to 5 inches long.

Red Efts are easy to see but hard to eat, and most predators avoid them. Their bright red skin gives off a poison that burns the mouth of animals that bite it.

The skin of Newts is rough and less slimy than the skin of other salamanders. Many male Newts are brightly colored. They usually develop a crest along the back and tail during breeding season.

Like many other eastern Newts, the Red-Spotted Newt hatches in a pond and moves onto land for 1 to 3 years. Then it returns to live in the same pond where it was born. During its time on land the Red-spotted Newt is called a Red Eft.

The Hellbender lives in clear, fast-flowing streams and rivers. It is from 12 to 29 inches long.

Giant Salamanders have large, flat bodies with folds of loose skin. They are born and live in the water. Their diet includes insects, crayfish, snails, fish eggs, and worms. Giant Salamanders are usually harmless, but they will bite if they are attacked.

The Giant Salamanders found in China and Japan can grow more than 5 feet in length and weigh as much as 50 pounds. They are the largest salamanders in the world. People sometimes catch Giant Salamanders and eat their meat. In North America, new dams and water pollution threaten their future.

The Three-toed Amphiuma is found in streams, swamps, and ditches in the South. It is from 18 to 42 inches long. It eats frogs, snakes, fish, and smaller Amphiumas.

Amphiumas (AM-fee-you-mus) have slippery bodies and look like eels. They are born and live in the water. Their four tiny legs are used only during the larval stage, when they help the larva move along the bottom of rivers and streams. Amphiumas may travel a short distance on land during wet weather.

The Lesser Siren is found along the southeast coast from Texas to South Carolina. It makes a clicking sound when excited and a faint yelping noise when captured.

Sirens have long bodies with two tiny front legs and are often mistaken for eels. They are born and live in the shallow water of swamps, weedy ponds, and ditches. Sirens keep their gills as they grow, and live their whole lives as larvae. They can reach up to 38½ inches in length, and eat plants, insect larvae, and other tiny animals.

The Mudpuppy is from 8 to 17 inches long and feeds on worms, crayfish, insects, and small fish. It is found in lakes, streams, and rivers from the Great Lakes south to Louisiana.

Mudpuppies and Waterdogs are born and live in the water. They do not grow past the larval stage and never lose their large bushy gills. Although they are named after animals that bark, Mudpuppies and Waterdogs are silent.

The Arboreal Salamander hunts insects on the ground and in the trees of the coastal mountains of California. It has been known to climb as high as 60 feet in search of food.

Lungless Salamanders breathe entirely through their skin. Most Lungless Salamanders are born in damp places on land and spend their lives on land. Unlike other salamanders, Lungless Salamanders usually do not desert their eggs. After laying them, Lungless Salamander females coil around their eggs, guarding them until they hatch.

The Cave Salamander lives in limestone caves and woodland springs. Helped along by a special long tail that can grasp rocks and ledges, the Cave Salamander climbs cave walls with ease, hunting for insects. It is 4½ to 7¼ inches long.

There are about 150 types of Lungless Salamanders, more than in any of the other salamander groups.

The Ensatina is the only salamander whose body is narrowed at the base of the tail. This is where the tail will break off when it is grabbed.

The Ensatina is a Lungless Salamander that is found along the Pacific coast. Like some other salamanders, the Ensatina stands stiff legged when threatened, showing its belly and swinging its arched tail.

If a predator grabs the tail of a salamander, the tail sometimes breaks off and wiggles about. This distracts the enemy while the salamander escapes. A new tail then grows back to replace the missing one. This is called regeneration.

Over the centuries, people have thought about salamanders in different ways.

An ancient myth of the Aztec people of Mexico tells the story of a god named Xolotl (EX-uh-lot-ell). Long ago, he dove deep into the water and changed himself into an axolotl (AX-uh-lot-ell) salamander when he was trying to escape from his enemies.

The emblem of Francis I, King of France in the early 1500s, was an imaginary creature that was part salamander and part dragon.

FIRE SALAMANDER

It was once thought that the Fire Salamander of Europe could eat fire and live in flames. Perhaps this idea came about when people noticed Fire Salamanders creeping away from logs tossed into fires. Stories were also told of salamanders turning into fire-breathing dragons.

The Fire Salamander can't eat fire, but it can aim and squirt a burning poison over 7 feet when it is annoyed. As with other animals that squirt poison, the spray drives predators away.

In _Macbeth_, the famous play written by William Shakespeare around 1606, the three witches say that they need "eye of newt" to perform their magic.

Hundreds of years ago, people tried to use salamanders to make medicines. They also believed that salamanders could help bring about magical changes, such as turning things into gold and making it possible for people to live much longer.

Today, scientists trying to understand how things grow are studying how the salamander regenerates missing body parts.

SPECKLED BLACK
SALAMANDER

Salamanders play an important role in the balance of nature. They help keep down the number of insects and other small creatures, and in turn become food for larger animals.

Because they take in both the air and the water through their skin, salamanders are sensitive to pollution. The building of dams, the filling of wetlands, acid rain, pesticides, and air pol-

CALIFORNIA
NEWT

lution are all harmful to salamanders. In some places, they have even become extinct. Many people think that tailed amphibians will not survive the changes in their environment.

The challenge facing salamanders may someday face all of us. We need to remember that living things need a balanced and healthy environment to survive.

Glossary

acid rain: Rain that has been made bitter by air pollution. It can harm plants and animals, especially in lakes and ponds.

algae (AL-jee): A plant-like material that grows without roots or leaves.

amphibian (am-FIB-ee-an): An animal with a backbone that has moist, unprotected skin and develops from a larva to an adult. Most spend time on land and in water.

arboreal (are-BORE-ee-uhl): Living in trees.

burrow: A hole or a tunnel dug by an animal for shelter.

camouflage (CAM-o-flaj): The coloring, marks, or shapes that hide an animal by making it look like a part of its surroundings.

breed: To mate or produce offspring.

cold-blooded: Having a body temperature that is the same as the surrounding temperature.

courtship: When male and female animals attract each other for mating.

extinct: When a type of plant or animal no longer exists in living form.

fertilize: To make certain changes in an egg so that it will develop into a baby.

gill: A breathing organ that takes oxygen from the water.

hatchling: An animal that has recently come out of its egg.

larva, larvae (plural): An amphibian in the first stage of life after hatching.

metamorphosis (met-uh-MOR-fuh-sis): The changes in an amphibian that take place from the larval to the adult stage.

pesticide (PEST-ih-side): A chemical used to destroy pests; it may also harm other animals.

predator: An animal that hunts and kills other animals for food.

regeneration (REE-jen-er-AY-shun): The regrowth of a body part that has been lost.

sperm: The substance given off by a male that can fertilize an egg when a male and a female mate.

wetland: A pond, swamp, tidal flat, or other damp area of land that is home to many kinds of plants and animals.